TAPEJARA

NOTHOSAURUS

TSINTAOSAURUS

CAUDIPTERYX

PACHYCEPHALOSAURUS

NEOVENATOR

KENTROSAURUS

OURANOSAURUS

ANTARCTOSAURUS

CHASMOSAURUS

JANE YOLEN

How Do Dinosaurs

Say I Love You?

Illustrated by

MARK TEAGUE

THE BLUE SKY PRESS

An Imprint of Scholastic Inc. • New York

THE BLUE SKY PRESS

SCHOLASTIC, THE BLUE SKY PRESS, and associated logos are

trademarks and/or registered trademarks of Scholastic Inc.

Library of Congress card catalog number: 2008049523

ISBN 13: 978-0-545-14314-1 / ISBN 10: 0-545-14314-4

20 19 18 17 16 15   17 18

Printed in Malaysia   108

First printing, October 2009

The artwork was created using acrylic paint.

Designed by Kathleen Westray

To wee dinosaur
David Stemple
J. Y.

To Mom
M. T.

You woke in the morning
in such a bad mood . . .

then sat at the table
and fussed with
your food.

But then you blew kisses
and waved from the door.
I love you, I love you,
my dinosaur.

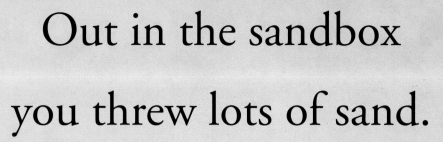

Out in the sandbox
you threw lots of sand.

CHASMOSAURUS

You ran from the slide,
after slapping
my hand.

But you suddenly turned
with a smile I adore.
Oh, I'll always
love you,
my dinosaur.

KENTROSAURUS

You moped through your nap time
and slept not a wink.

You flooded the house when you played in the sink.

But you got out the mop
and then cleaned
up the floor!
I love you
so much,
little dinosaur.

ANTARCTOSAURUS

Off in the car,
you kept kicking

my seat . . .

and when we got out,
you were dragging
your feet.

But you held my hand tight
when we walked in the store.
I'll love you forever,
my dinosaur.

Dinner disaster!

You made such a mess!

Would you stay up past bedtime?

The answer was

YES!

But when you smile sweetly
and hold back your roar,
when you kiss me and hug me
once, twice, even more . . .

. . . that's when you give love,
and I know this is true,
because *that's* how a dinosaur says
I Love You!

NOTHOSAURUS

TSINTAOSAURUS

TAPEJARA

CAUDIPTERYX

PACHYCEPHALOSAURUS

NEOVENATOR

KENTROSAURUS

OURANOSAURUS

ANTARCTOSAURUS

CHASMOSAURUS